"Ahoy mateys! I be Captain Barnacle," said the old pirate as we entered the aquarium. "I have a whale of a tale to tell ye about me days at sea, fighting ruthless pirates and fierce waves, while searching for me lost treasure."

"Ahoy mateys!" repeated his parrot.

We followed the captain into the first exhibit.
"Here you'll see countless species of fish. Many of these aquatic, cold-blooded vertebrates I discovered on me journey," said the captain.

Fish are vertebrates, meaning they have a backbone. They live in water, and most of them breathe through gills, have scales, and swim with fins.

There are over 27,000 different kinds of fish.

"With only me treasure map, me compass, and me parrot, I sailed the ocean blue, searching high and low for me treasure."
"High and low!" repeated the parrot.

Water is not all the same. The ocean is salt water while most lakes and rivers are fresh water. Some fish can survive in both but many live only in salt or fresh water.

Fish breathe through gills on the sides of their heads. They take in water through their mouths and remove the oxygen when the water passes over their gills. A fish uses its nose to smell, not to breathe.

Fish have a mucous coating to help them move through the water and to protect them from diseases—that's why they feel slimy.

An ichthyologist is a person who studies fish.

Fixed on the captain's every word,
we followed him into the shark exhibit.
"I encountered many scary critters, such
as the sharks ye see here," he said. "The first
clue on me map was a shark, so I sailed
me ship fearlessly toward
shark-infested waters."

Sharks

Sharks have existed for over
400 million years, even before
dinosaurs. Most sharks have
5 to 6 rows of teeth, which
replace themselves often.

"The sharks surrounded me ship. I was sure I'd be their grub when, unexpectedly, the sharks attacked some nearby eels—a tastier treat than an old salty pirate like meself.

"'Shiver me timbers!' I hollered. 'That was close!'"

"Shiver me timbers!" repeated the parrot.

The Great White Shark is one of the largest sharks. It can grow up to 21 feet long (6.4 meters) and weigh over 2 tons.

Sharks can be found in fresh water, but most live in the ocean.

Eels

Eels are fish that are snakelike in shape and can be found in sea and fresh water. Eels release a layer of slime over their bodies to protect themselves from getting cuts and to help them move around in the water.

We walked closely behind the captain into the next room.

"I sailed for days with no sign of land or me treasure, when, out of the blue, dolphins appeared.

"'Avast!' I said to the dolphins. 'Have ye seen me lost treasure?'

"'The sword marks the spot,' one whistled and clicked.

"'What does that mean?' I asked them. But they swam away without uttering another sound."

"Sword marks the spot!" repeated the parrot, as we followed the captain to the next exhibit.

Dolphins

Dolphins are mammals, not fish. They cannot breathe under water. They swim to the surface to get air through a hole on the top of their heads called a blowhole. They can hold their breath for approximately 10 minutes and can dive as deep as 1,000 feet (304 meters).

Dolphins communicate with one another through whistles, clicking, and tail slapping. Scientists believe each dolphin has its own unique whistle.

There have been reports that some dolphins have put their own safety at risk to protect other dolphins, sea creatures, and even humans.

Barnacles

Barnacles are crustaceans, animals that live in a hard shell. They are invertebrates—no backbone. They attach themselves to rocks and bottoms of boats.

"I sailed on, searching for any sign of a sword, when I encountered a mighty blue whale—another symbol on me map. The gigantic critter swam so close to me ship that he tossed me to and fro until I crashed on a nearby beach!"

Whales

Like dolphins, whales are mammals, not fish. They cannot breathe under water. They each have a blowhole on the top of their head for breathing. Whales live in the ocean.

"'Blow me down!' I hollered at the whale. 'I'll never find me treasure without me ship!' I cried." "Blow me down!" repeated the parrot.

Blue whales are the largest mammal ever to live on the earth. They are even larger than dinosaurs. They can grow to a length of 100 feet (30 meters) and weigh as much as 160 tons.

Whales are among the loudest animals on earth—their moans, groans, and squeaks can be heard many miles away.

"With no hope of rescue, I looked around for something to make a raft, when I came across an old sign in the sand. It read, 'Gone Fishing!'

"'Sword marks the spot!' squawked me parrot."

Swordfish

Swordfish are one of the fastest fish. They can swim as fast as 60 miles per hour (96 kilometers per hour). They can live for 10 years or longer and weigh as much as 1,200 pounds.

Crabs

Crabs are crustaceans with 10 legs and a hard shell. The shell protects them from attackers.

Lobsters

Lobsters are crustaceans. They shed their hard shells and grow new ones as they get bigger.

"'Blimey!' I yelled in surprise.
Could it be that this sign was
the clue the dolphin told to me?
"'Sword marks the spot.'
repeated me parrot."

Gone Fishing!

Shrimp

Shrimp are crustaceans.
They are found all around the
world in fresh and salt water.

Stonefish

The Reef Stonefish is a very poisonous fish that lives on the ocean floor. Its sand-colored, bumpy skin helps it to hide in its surroundings.

Starfish

A starfish is not actually a fish; it has no fins or gills. Its has hundreds of tiny suction-cup feet that propel it through water.

"...and dig..."

Gone Fishing!

"...and dig some more, when at last me shovel hit something hard."

Sponges

There are around 5,000 different species of sponges. They come in all shapes, sizes, and colors.

Clams

Clams live in sand and mud on the seashore. They are made up of two outer shells hinged together and muscles. The muscles allow a clam to open and close and its foot allows it to burrow in the sand.

"It was me loot!

"I opened it up. It was filled with glittering gold, silver, and jewels. I began to sing and dance—Yo-ho-ho!"

"But me excitement ended when jellyfish washed ashore and stung me foot. 'Ouch!' I hollered."

"Ouch!" repeated the parrot.

Jellyfish

Jellyfish have been on the earth for 540 million years. They have no heart, brain, or bones. They defend themselves from predators by stinging them.

"I grabbed me loot and paddled away as fast as I could."

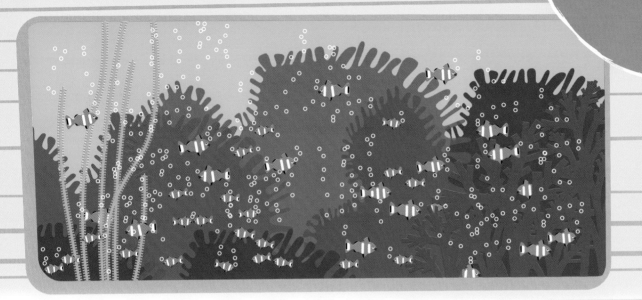

Clown Fish

Clown fish come in many colors. The most common is the orange-with-white-stripes variety. They live in warm water in the Pacific Ocean, the Red Sea, the Indian Ocean, and in Australia's Great Barrier Reef.

Dwarf Goby

The Dwarf Goby is one of the smallest fish in the ocean. They grow to less than a half inch (1.2 centimeters).

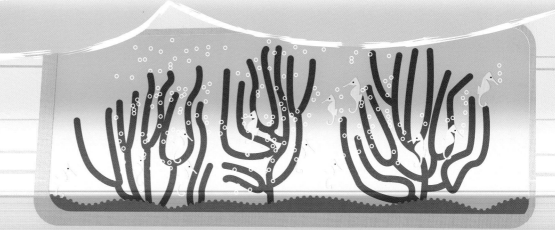

"Cast out to sea with nothing but me small raft and me treasure, I encountered a ship of evil pirates. "'Surrender ye treasure!' threatened the pirates."

Sea Horses

Sea horses propel themselves by a dorsal fin on their backs. They are the slowest fish in the sea. The male gives birth to the babies instead of the female.

"With no way to escape, I put me hands up in surrender. Me end was near, when suddenly the biggest squid I'd ever seen came from the bottom of the sea, wrapped his tentacles around the hull of the pirate's ship, and sank it. Me life was saved!"

Giant Squid

The giant squid lives in the ocean but has never been seen alive. It is among the largest creatures in the sea. It has a torpedo-shaped body with 8 tentacles and 2 long feeding arms. The giant squid can grow up to 60 feet long (18 meters) and can weigh over one ton.

"I continued on home, singing, 'Yo-ho-ho!'"
"Yo-ho-ho!" repeated the parrot.

"So, me hearties, the long and short of it be this—I got home safely and opened me aquarium with me loot."

Captain Barnacle

Parrot

The Marlin

"Come again soon, me mateys!" said Captain Barnacle as he quickly ushered us out the exit.
"Come again soon, me mateys!" repeated the parrot.

PIRATE TERMS

ahoy—hello

avast!—hey!

aye—yes

blimey!—an exclamation of surprise

grub—food

landlubber—a person who lives on land or a sailor on his first voyage

loot—treasure

me—my or mine

me hearties—what a captain calls his crew

shiver me timbers!—an expression of surprise or strong emotion

old salt—a name for an experienced seaman

ye—you

yo-ho-ho—a common phrase a pirate sings

Many thanks to Dr. Lawrence M. Page, Ichthyologist and Curator of Fishes at the Florida Museum of Natural History, University of Florida; Dr. Lance Morgan, Chief Scientist of the Marine Conservation Biology Institute; and Jennifer Fiegl of the National Aquarium in Baltimore for contributing their expert knowledge of marine life.—E. M.

To my art teacher,
Florence McCarthy
—E. M.

Harry N. Abrams, Inc.
115 West 18th Street, New York, NY 10011

Abrams is a subsidiary of
LA MARTINIÈRE
GROUPE